THE EYE OF THE NEEDLE

retold and illustrated by Teri Sloat

based on a Yupik tale as told by Betty Huffmon

A PUFFIN UNICORN

PUFFIN UNICORN BOOKS

Published by the Penguin Group
Penguin Books USA Inc., 375 Hudson Street, New York, New York 10014, U.S.A.
Penguin Books Ltd, 27 Wrights Lane, London W8 5TZ, England
Penguin Books Australia Ltd, Ringwood, Victoria, Australia
Penguin Books Canada Ltd, 10 Alcorn Avenue, Toronto, Ontario, Canada M4V 3B2
Penguin Books (N.Z.) Ltd, 182-190 Wairau Road, Auckland 10, New Zealand
Penguin Books Ltd, Registered Offices: Harmondsworth, Middlesex, England

Library of Congress number 89-49476
ISBN 0-14-054933-1

Published in the United States by Dutton Children's Books,
a division of Penguin Books USA Inc.
Designer: Riki Levinson
Printed in Hong Kong by South China Printing Co.
First Puffin Unicorn Edition 1993
1 3 5 7 9 10 8 6 4 2

THE EYE OF THE NEEDLE is also available in hardcover
from Dutton Children's Books.

to Betty Huffmon, my favorite storyteller

TERI SLOAT

Betty Huffmon

Long ago, on the shore of the cold sea, Little Amik lived with his grandmother in a tiny sod hut.

It was the time between the dark of winter and the warmth of summer, and there was little left to eat. Amik and his grandmother waited for the sun to melt the ice and for the spring breeze to send it from the shore. Then they could gather food from the sea once again.

Grandmother sat inside the hut, sewing with a beautiful ivory needle. Her eyes were old, but the wide, open eye of her needle helped her see many things.

One day, when Grandmother knew the ice was ready to leave, she spoke.

"Little Amik, I have been watching you grow. This spring, you are big enough to go out and hunt our food for us."

The next morning,
Amik dressed quickly in
his newly mended spring
parka and hurried to the
shore.

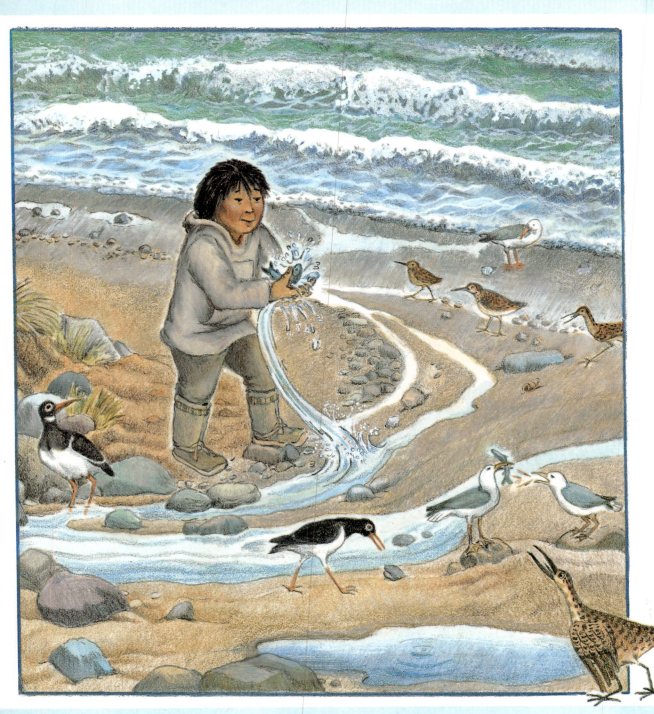

In a stream trickling past his feet, something flickered across the pebbles. Amik scooped up a tiny needlefish.

"I am so hungry," he said. "I will eat this and catch something bigger for Grandmother." And with that...

...he popped the spiny
needlefish into his mouth.
"Glump."
Down
went the
needlefish.
A moment later, Amik
said, "I am still hungry."

As Amik followed the shore, a squirmy hooligan fish flopped at his feet. He reached into the water and grabbed its slippery sides.

"I am so hungry," he said. "I will eat this and catch something bigger for Grandmother." And with that ...

"Gulump."

Down
    slipped the
        hooligan.

But a moment later, Amik said, "I am still hungry."

A few steps ahead, noisy seagulls swooped over salmon in a little river.

Amik scattered the birds with a handful of pebbles. Catching a salmon by the tail, he licked his lips and said, "I am *so* hungry. I will eat this and catch something bigger for Grandmother." And with that...

Amik opened his mouth wide and...

"GULLUMP."

Down

slid the

salmon.

But only a moment later, he said, "I am STILL hungry!"

Amik hurried along the
beach, eating more and
more but growing
hungrier and hungrier.

Soon he came upon a
fat seal resting on the
sand. Amik thought how
his grandmother loved
seal. But he said, "I am SO
hungry. I will eat this and
catch something bigger
for Grandmother." And
with that . . .

...he lifted the seal, stretched his mouth open wide, and...

"GULLUMMP!"
Down
flipped the
seal.

But within a moment, Amik said, "I am STILL hungry!"

And on down the beach he went, in search of more food.

Not far ahead, a lazy
walrus slept on the rocks,
basking in the warm sun.
Amik crept up close.

While the walrus slept, Amik grasped him by his long, ivory tusks. "Grandmother would be proud of this catch," he said. "But I am SO hungry. I will wait to catch something even bigger for Grandmother." And with that...

He lifted the walrus from the rocks, opened his mouth wider than ever, and...

"GULLUUMMP!"
    Down
        wriggled the
            walrus.

After he jiggled the walrus into a comfortable spot, Amik said, "I am STILL hungry!"

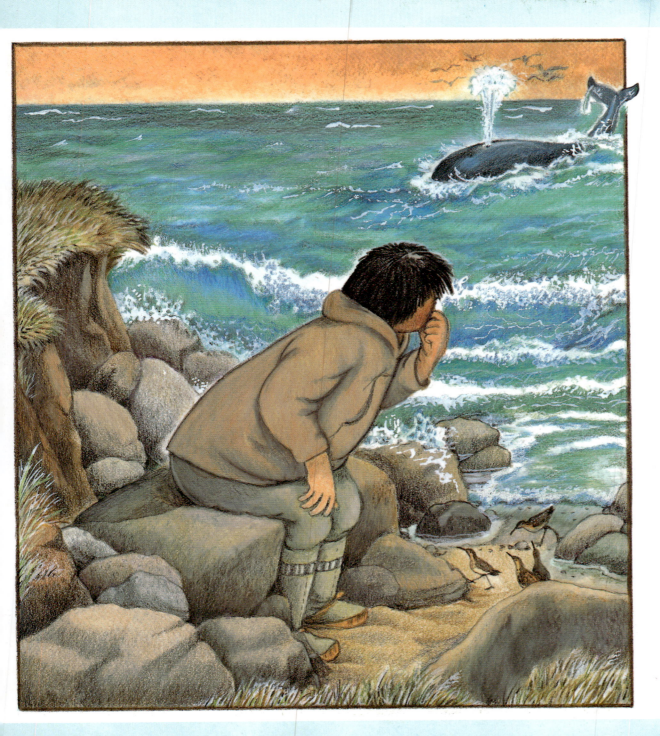

Out on the water, Amik saw the prize of the sea, a great whale! Here was a creature with enough meat to feed an entire village for a whole winter.

To Amik the whale looked very tasty indeed.

Amik watched the whale glide in on the crest of a wave. "I am so hungry," he said, without one thought of his grandmother. And with that...

He bent down low and opened his mouth to an enormous size. When the wave rolled in to crash on the sand...

"G-U-L-L-U-U-M-M-P!"
Down
rushed the
WHALE!
After a moment, Amik said, "I am NOT hungry!"

"But I AM very thirsty."
Stopping at the nearest
stream, he slurped swallow
after swallow until the
stream was dry.

Then Amik took a long,
long rest.

When he awoke, Amik remembered he had saved nothing for his grandmother.

Too tired and much too full to hunt, Amik plodded slowly back to the hut, wondering what to tell Grandmother.

When Grandmother heard Amik outside, she called, "Come in with your catch, Amik. I am *so* hungry."

Amik was very uncomfortable. "But, Grandmother, my catch is much too big to bring through the door."

Grandmother was
sewing with her ivory
needle. "You must have
returned with many things
for us, Amik. Climb to
the top of the hut and
come in through the
smoke hole."

Amik knew the smoke hole was much smaller even than the doorway. But he always did what his grandmother told him, so he pulled himself to the top of the hut before he asked, "How am I to squeeze through such a small hole?"

"Now you can come in through the eye of my needle," she replied.

Amik groaned. "Grandmother, the eye of your needle is many times smaller than the smoke hole."

But as soon as Grandmother held the needle up to the smoke hole, Amik was magically drawn into the hut.

As he slid through the needle into the hut, there was a loud "POP!" Then a rush of water swirled him around and around.

Out came

"SWISH!" Out slipped the

"SWOOSH!" Out slid the *salmon.*

"SPLASH!" Out flipped the *seal.*

"WHOOSH!" Out wriggled the *walrus.*

he needlefish, past Grandmother's nose.
ooligan fish.

And they all flowed out of the hut.

Then with a great "RUMBLE!"...
out on a wave rolled the whale.

Out of the whale came shrimp, seaweed, crabs, fish eggs,

and even a whaling ship in full sail.

When everything came to rest, Grandmother said, "Amik, what a wonderful provider you are."

Grandmother enjoyed a fine feast. Then she proudly shared their catch with all who came to see them. Amik did not eat—he was no longer hungry.